FOREST
OF
FAITH

God's Love Is a WARM COOKIE

Sharing with Others Is Sweet as Can Be

by Susan Jones

Illustrated by Lee Holland

Good Books

New York, New York

One morning, Little Hedgehog
wakes up to a curious sound.

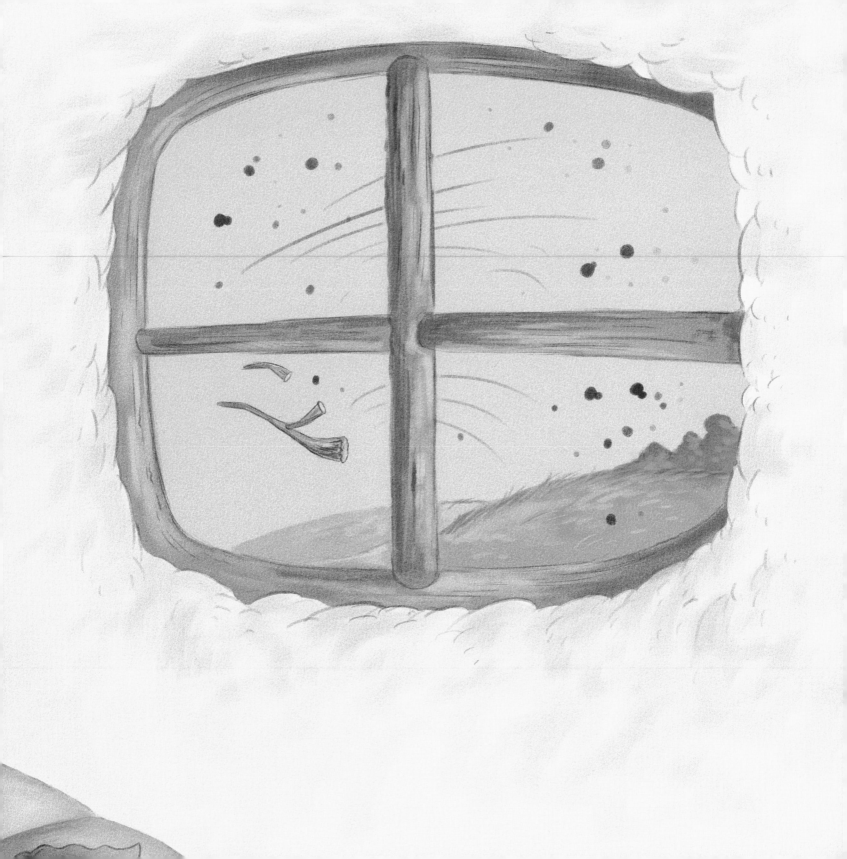

Outside, a family of bunnies is digging a brand-new burrow.

"New neighbors! And one is as small as me," Little Hedgehog says, running into the kitchen.

"You should go say hello," says Mama.

But Little Hedgehog is too shy to go.

"I won't know what to say,"
Little Hedgehog squeaks.

"Bring them a welcome gift that says
the words you can't," suggests Mama.

"What's that thing you always say about God's love?" asks Little Hedgehog as she grabs a paper and pencil.

"It's in our hearts. When we give to others from our hearts," says Mama, "we share God's love."

"I know just what to do," says
Little Hedgehog.

"Where are you going?"
asks Mama, but Little
Hedgehog is already
skipping away.

"You wanna go to the field and *fly* a kite?" asks Little Raccoon.

"No, thanks," says Little Hedgehog.
"I need to get some eggs."

EGGS
FOR
SALE

"Come *fishing* with me!" says
Little Fox.

"Sounds fun. But I really need to get milk!" replies Little Hedgehog.

"That's a lot of stuff you're carrying. Want a lift, Little Hedgehog?" asks Grandma Turtle.

"No thanks. I've got this,"
she says.

"The berries are ripe and sweet," says Little Deer. "Care to try a *few*?"

"Not today," Little Hedgehog squeaks, though her belly *is* growling.

"I'm ready to make my welcome gift!" says Little Hedgehog.

"We'll help," offer Mama and Papa.

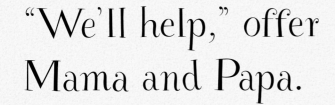

They mix.

And roll.

And cut.

And bake.

Ding! The smell of fresh cookies fills the air.

"You can do it," says Mama.

So Little Hedgehog, with her heart beating fast, carries the cookies to her new neighbors.

"For me?" asks Little Bunny. "This is the perfect welcome gift."

And just like that, they know they will be wonderful friends.

The delicious scent of cookies brings all the animals together for a welcome party.

Soon, their bellies are *full* of the cookies they shared, and their hearts are *full* of God's love.

THE BUNNY FAM

Little Hedgehog's Sugar Cookies

Follow the recipe below to make Little Hedgehog's special cookies. What makes these cookies so sweet? The act of sharing with others. Whom will you share God's love with today?

Yield: 3 dozen cookies

Ingredients

1 cup butter (2 sticks), softened
¾ cup sugar
1 large egg
½ teaspoon vanilla extract

2½ cups all-purpose flour
¼ teaspoon baking soda
¼ teaspoon salt

Directions

1) Preheat oven to 375°F.
2) Beat butter, sugar, egg, and vanilla together in a large mixing bowl.
3) Combine the remaining ingredients and add them slowly to the egg mixture. Beat on low until combined.
3) Form the dough into a ball using your hands. Wrap the dough and let it cool for 30 minutes in the refrigerator.

4) Lightly flour your surface and roll out half of the dough until it is about ¼ of an inch thick. Use your cookie cutters to cut the dough into shapes like hearts, doves, and crosses. Place cut cookies 1 inch apart on an ungreased cookie sheet.
5) Bake for 6-8 minutes or until cookies begin to brown at the edges. Transfer to a wire rack to cool.
6) Top with your favorite frosting and a dash of sprinkles for extra sweetness!

Visit our website at www.goodbooks.com.

10 9 8 7 6 5 4 3 2 1

Library of Congress Cataloging-in-Publication Data is available on file.

Cover illustration by Lee Holland

Print ISBN: 978-1-68099-570-1
Ebook ISBN: 978-1-68099-573-2

Printed in China